THE LIGHT OF LIGHTS

RULES OF VENGEANCE, THE BEGINNING

GIACOMO GIAMMATTEO

INFERNO PUBLISHING COMPANY

Print ISBN 978-1-940313-60-3

Electronic ISBN 978-1-940313-59-7

❀ Created with Vellum

INTRODUCTION

This is the beginning of the Rules of Vengeance. It provides some backstory on what happened prior to everyone being exiled. The story takes place in another part of the universe, where some people have special abilities (genetically inherited), and there are other weapons that can be used for warfare.

In this section of the universe, there are seven worlds that are inhabited by races of people who have lived there for thousands of years. Now, the worlds are at war.

With that said, welcome to the seven worlds of Nelstar.

STORMS OF WAR

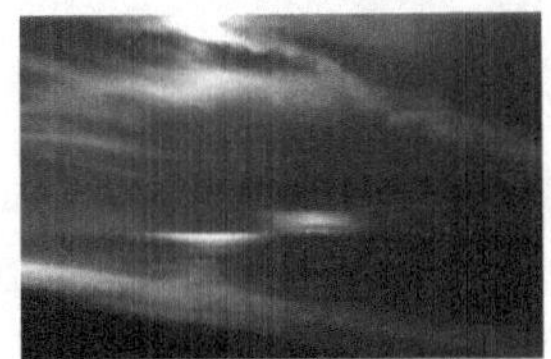

Savar, Fourth World in the Nelstar System
739 AD (After Darkness)
Second Cycle of the Third Moon
Second Calendar of Light

*W*here are they? They should have returned by now. Antar's racing heart constricted. *What images will they bring? What horrors?*

Stepping from shadows to the glare of morning sun, Antar's long strides carried him past marble columns as wide as a man is tall and mahogany shelves crowded with ancient leather-bound tomes. When he turned, his black cape swirled, flinging motes of dust into a chaotic dance.

Where are they?

He plucked a book from the shelf and, for the third time, forced himself to sit. A frown appeared while browsing through a treatise on double envelopment, a military tactic he had used during the Wars of Darkness. It had been a long time since they had fought wars where that tactic meant much. Now, men died in droves and few, if any, carried swords. The only steel weapons were tainted with poison and hidden in assassins' cloaks.

Antar focused on the soothing shores of Lake Mago, then the springs near the Endoran coast, though nothing kept his mind from racing, from wondering what images the *slicers* would bring. He should have done this long ago. It had been too long since he had dared to look. Since—

He straightened, unfolded his hands, and shut the book with a clap. The first *slicer* flew over the Sorrelan Sea, racing toward the mainland. Within a few heartbeats, he sensed the others. Of all the Blood, only he could sense a *slicer*. He placed the book on the table and stood to receive the news. The *slicers*—slivers of crystal as thin as a hair—slid into the room as if the walls weren't there, ushered in by streaks of sunlight.

Lenorda

With the first image Antar's heart sank. Lenorda, the third world, lay in ruins: buildings crumbled, ships aflame in the harbors, and bodies sprawled along streets and walks. He shook his head as reports arrived from other worlds. *How many must die?*

A tear escaped from the corner of his eye, then a lump of pity choked his throat when an image of his long-dead son flashed before him.

I should never have used the Sacred Book.

He turned to see Molina entering the room with khaffe. She knew what he needed, and when. The strong aroma calmed him, made him reach for the mug. He would need this and many more cups before the day was done. "You should see... No, you shouldn't. No one should. But I must do something..."

"I won't shut my eyes to this. You'll show me tonight, but for now, relax." Molina shared the khaffe with him, then she reached for his hand. "Come, dear, let's walk. You could use the distraction and, besides, the children are playing. We could both use a smile."

"I should stay."

"And do what? There is nothing more you can do."

Antar pounded the table with his fist. "I can't relax with all of this going on."

Molina stared, her hand still extended.

A long pause preceded a reluctant nod. "Forgive me, dear, you're right. I could use the smile."

Antar and Molina strolled hand-in-hand through the gardens of Manor du Savarra, their love still as strong as his grip, even after so many centuries. Fifty hectares of land surrounded the mansion, one of many in this part of the city. The manor served as a veritable paradise for the orphans Antar and Molina sheltered, most of them victims of the war.

Antar's manor

Small children frolicked and hid behind manicured hedges, chasing each other like wolf cubs through red-tipped ligustrums and crape myrtles. The older children played among the old oaks that guarded the gates and shaded the walks, their huge branches serving as stages for re-enactments of legendary sword fights.

Antar watched them play, remembering a time when his children spent their days there. The memories carried warmth to his heart, replaced the sorrow with love.

He knelt next to a flowering dogwood that was balanced on a spindly leg and called to one of the little orphan boys. White blossoms shined next to Antar's black hair and olive skin. "Torne, come here."

Torne raced to him, smile turning to laughter even before he reached Antar. "What do you have?" he asked, hand outstretched.

"Nothing…unless I can coax a hug from you."

Torne wrapped his arms around Antar's neck and squeezed, then stood back, his brown eyes searching for the prize.

From behind his back, Antar produced several *cormas*, hard candies made with a blend of peppermint.

Torne snatched them from Antar's hand with a laugh, then turned to run, a gleam still in his eyes.

"Remember to share those with your friends," Antar said as Torne darted away.

Antar glanced back at Molina, his hand reaching for hers. "He reminds me so much of our son, though it's difficult to remember when he was that young." A gentle caress accompanied his smile, just his thumb touching the back of her hand.

"I remember when he was that wild," Molina said. She sighed as she leaned against Antar's shoulder, long tresses of dark hair cushioning her head. "If only they could stay this innocent."

Antar buried his face in her locks, nudged her hair aside, then let his lips find the nape of her neck. Her hair had been the first thing he noticed when they met so long ago. Black as a raven's wing and silky as a *seglar's* weave. With a deep breath he savored the smell, like lavender in her warm baths. And that brought other times to mind. Precious times.

While he was stroking Molina's hair, she pointed to a servant approaching at a run.

"It's Benna! Something must be wrong."

Benna arrived, still panting from his race across the manor. "Master, one of our scouts in the southern range reported a storm coming. It moved a full quadrant since dawn."

Antar focused his gaze on the thunderheads looming in the distance. A full quadrant since dawn was far too fast for a typical storm.

Molina gripped his arm, and her dark eyes froze. "It's him again, isn't it?"

"We will see soon enough." A *slicer* emerged from a pouch hanging at Antar's side and sped toward the roiling mass in the center of the blackness, still many leagues away. It returned within moments.

Antar let go of Molina's hand, then focused, issuing a warning that radiated to minds throughout the city:

"Get the children to shelter. Hurry!"

He dispatched more *slicers* to strategic points across the city, then closed his eyes to focus again. Mothers and fathers screamed, snatching babies up in their arms while they dragged older children by the hands or wrists, anything to rush them to safety.

Molina raced to a young girl playing with her cat. "Come, baby. Hurry!" She grabbed both of them in her arms. "Benna, make sure all the children get in," she hollered, legs pumping as she ran toward the house.

Rolling in from the south, the thunderheads moved ever faster. A *slicer* returned with fresh images, digging a deeper frown on Antar's face. Time was running short. "Benna, tell Jarrell to reinforce the shields. They're not holding in the south. I'll contact the other guards." He reached out to every quadrant. *"Join together and shield the children. Quickly!"*

storm

Thunder cracked and lightning struck. Shields collapsed against the assault like stiff-backed pines in a Gorshan Storm. Benna directed parents and children and any other stray by the quickest route, guiding them to safety under the aegis of Antar's shield. "Master, hurry. It is too close now." Though half blind, Benna still knew these gardens like an old dog knows the dark.

Antar sent out a message for all to hear. *"Abandon your defenses. Retreat to the manor."*

Antar studied the storm a moment longer—as long as he dared—then rushed to the manor. He had fused his house with a shield when he built it, but he knew this would be a ferocious attack and prayed the house would hold. The door closed behind him just as the assault began.

"Jarrell!" His stentorian shout rang in every room, bringing the commander of the guard within heartbeats. Still shaking, but now with vengeance, Antar instructed Jarrell. "Mount a counterattack.

They'll be hiding behind the clouds in the high grounds. I want them found."

Fire danced in his eyes as he clenched both fists. "I want them *destroyed*."

Rage had a firm grip on Antar now. Lukaan had gone too far. It was one thing to wage a war, but to endanger the children… Suddenly it struck him. Where was Torne? He raced to the front door, saw Kena, the gardener's wife, with her two-year-old son wrapped in her arms, and another child alongside her. Panic seized his heart.

That's Torne.

He flung the front doors open and sent a thought to her as he ran. *"Run, Kena."*

A bolt of *blacklightning* shattered the stone wall to his side. Another felled his favorite chestnut tree, crashing it to the ground in front of him. He leapt aside, dodging the tree.

"Hurry!" Energy coalesced, particles fusing into a shield over Kena and Torne. Three bolts of *blacklightning* smashed the shield before he completed it, rending it apart. Tearing through the rift, another blast struck Kena and Torne.

"No… No!" Antar's gut twisted. Lightning cracked on all sides of him, one bolt singeing his arm. "Not Torne."

He fused another shield, then knelt beside them.

Dead. Torne's stomach was ripped apart, the remains a charred mass of flesh. Antar picked up Kena's baby and Torne, cradling them in his arms as lightning pummeled the shield.

Propping himself on one knee, he focused on his defenses, weaving a tight net. He stood on shaky legs, then made his way toward the house. Another barrage struck. Antar fell, Torne's body slipping from his arms as he fought to remain conscious. Blood trickled from his ear.

It was Lukaan. Only Lukaan was strong enough to do this.

Ten of Antar's personal guards raced from the house, shields forming into dome-shaped structures of energy to fend off the assault.

Jarrell grabbed Kena's baby, but when he reached for Torne, Antar's glare met him.

"Lord Antar, we cannot hold the shield for long."

Antar struggled to his feet, clutching Torne's body as if it were life itself. "Get Kena," he said, then hurried to the manor. Lightning trailed him to the entrance.

Molina flung the doors open just before he arrived. Anxiety wore heavy on her face—jaw tight, teeth clenched.

"Are you all right?" she asked.

"Fine."

"Torne, is he…?"

"Gone," Antar said, shaking his head.

She unfolded his arms and took Kena's baby. "His father will need healing."

"How could I forget!" Antar snapped at her with angry eyes, felt the flames eating his tears.

A gentle touch from Molina calmed him. He focused, regulated his breathing to cool his temperature. "I will be there soon for healing."

Molina walked away with the baby's body while Antar clung to Torne's remains.

Benna stood beside him. His cheeks were as gaunt as a starving man, but his belly betrayed him with a plumpness reserved for those who ate well, and often. "Master, let me take him. I'll make khaffe while you wash." The servant reached for the boy but stopped short at his master's reaction.

"No! We cannot send him away like this." Antar clutched Torne's body against his chest.

Benna cleared a table and covered it with an old sheet.

Antar nodded, then laid Torne on the table. He worked deft hands across the boy's body, a soft blue light permeating the skin until it drew closed, sealing the gaping hole.

Benna gasped when the body moved, but a soft touch from Antar alleviated the fear.

"No need to worry. I am not a Maker." He stared down at Torne, stroking the boy's hair. "If only I were…"

He picked Torne up, then a long silence followed before Antar spoke. "What do we do, Benna? He has no parents to weep for him."

"He has us." Benna pried Antar's long fingers open one at a time, then unwrapped Antar's arms and lifted Torne's body. "I will care for him, Master."

Antar nodded, wiped his face with his sleeve, then strode to the window to renew his vigilance. All around him thunder cracked, and lightning plummeted from the dark sky. It ripped walls from foundations, collapsed structures, and shattered buildings. A tree spiraled on a torrent of wind, crashing into the house across the Way.

destruction of city

Antar focused his power on a new shield. Veins bulged as pressure built in his head. He had spread himself too thin.

Moments later, a keening streak of *blacklightning* struck the wall of the house across from him, ripped it from its foundation. Antar buckled under the strain, but he maintained the shield. He refused to allow more deaths. Not today. Not ever again.

At the other end of the room, servants huddled with strangers from across the city. "What do we do?" a cook asked Benna.

"Wait it out. There is little else to do. But try not to worry, my dear. We are as safe here as any can be." Benna patted the servant's back as he spoke.

The assault raged throughout the rest of the morning and early afternoon, wreaking destruction in every quadrant for leagues. Antar dispatched *slicers* to scout the city. By late afternoon the fury subsided. The madness ceased.

Once the calm had been restored, and the others had been fed, Benna brought soup for Molina and Antar. More khaffe, too. "Three attacks with no warning, Master. They have found a way around your safeguards."

Antar pushed the soup away, though he accepted the cup of khaffe. His trembling hands wrapped around the mug like a cold man seeking warmth. "He will pay for this, Benna. They all will pay."

Steam curled at Antar's lip as he took another sip. "Feed everybody. Tell them to stay as long as necessary."

Benna nodded and turned to leave, but Antar called him back. "What did you do with Torne?"

"His body is safe, Master. Nothing can get to it. I'll have the grave marker start in the morning."

"Lay him next to my son. There is an empty plot there."

A smile lit Benna's face. His blue eyes widened before misting. "Yes, Master... Anything else?"

"Tell Jarrell to gather the men. We need to search for survivors. Find them shelter. Bring them here if need be...and, Benna, tell Kena's husband I will heal him now."

Molina waited until Benna left, then stared into Antar's eyes. "We have got to stop Lukaan. Billions will die if we don't." She finished her khaffe then wiped a tear from her eye. "What can we do when he refuses to battle with honor? How do we fight a war like this?"

With grim determination Antar stroked the scars that experience had carved on his face—a gash under the right eye, and a spot along his left jawline where a beard refused to grow. "I will find him, Molina. There are only seven worlds where he can hide."

DANGEROUS ASPIRATIONS

*L*ukaan sat upon a makeshift throne, veins protruding like swollen rivers from the back of large hands that gripped the polished marble armrests. He remembered the Darkness, that long and bitter struggle, but he remembered, too, how Antar had stopped him from using the Sacred Book.

A tinge of red darkened his bronzed face, and a jaw like a blacksmith's anvil clenched strong teeth. Antar would pay for that treachery. It had taken one hundred years but he would pay now.

Lukaan stood, walked toward Ghruehne. Lukaan was tall, even for a Runellan, with broad shoulders and a face defined by strong bones. A careful smile nudged the corner of his lips toward burnt brown eyes smoldering with hatred. Lukaan's gaze held Ghruehne in place. "Well?"

Ghruehne swallowed, the lump in his throat retracting as he gulped. He stood tall enough to look Lukaan in the eyes, but he did not have the courage for that. His heart was as soft as his skin. He clenched his fists then raised his eyes, but only to Lukaan's chin. "He escaped again." A plea for absolution dripped from his words.

A false smile darted across Lukaan's face. "You let Antar get away after what he did to you?" He knew that fires yet raged inside of Ghruehne, burning since the assault near the Parakhan Sea had marred his beautiful face. Lightning had gouged a mark as red as Ghruehne's hair from ear to eye. Since then, vengeance and Ghruehne had become fast friends.

Ghruehne's face twisted into a scowl, his left eye twitching where the scar was. "Antar's manor is impenetrable; besides, no matter where he is, he can shift when he sees a storm." Ghruehne shook his head. "So why the attacks? It makes no sense."

"He won't expect us to try again so soon. Not an attack of this type. And remember, I know what he cares about. He would dive to the bottom of the Gorshan Sea to save Aentarra. She's the most precious of his daughters."

"You captured Aentarra?"

"No, but Antar doesn't know that. And we have reports that she is on Endora, two worlds away. Too far for him to verify so quickly."

Ripples formed in the air, like a gentle breeze on a pond, then a rift opened. Vellana stepped through. She nodded to Lukaan, ignored Ghruehne. "I bear a message from Council, and it's for your ears only."

Lukaan's gaze lingered on Vellana's soft curves. He held no desire for her, but the allure was undeniable; men were forced to stare. "Leave us, Ghruehne."

Vellana waited for Ghruehne to depart, though her focus never left Lukaan. "Council does not approve of your plan. We cannot sanction it."

"Cowards, all of you. My way will ensure victory. Antar is nothing without Molina."

"If you … did what you had intended with her, there would be no stopping him. With our plan we can force him to take the Oath."

"It's a coward's way to win a war. I can defeat him."

Vellana's face turned crimson, blotches forming on her arms. "You have tried for one hundred years. How long do you need? How much is enough?"

Weak to the core they are. Afraid. "All five voted for this?"

"Unanimous," she said, and smiled.

Lukaan nodded. "I will get her tonight. But be prepared for his fury."

A frown replaced her smile. "Just make certain no one harms her." She wagged a finger at Lukaan. "Not a scratch. If she is dishonored…"

"Leave me, Vellana, before I forget we are allies. And tell Sendra that I need her."

Vellana's blue eyes sparkled. "A good idea, fellow Light. Rid yourself of all your passions before you visit Molina."

A distortion in the air ushered Vellana from the room. A moment later another disturbance opened a rift, allowing Sendra to enter. She bowed to Lukaan, head held low.

Lukaan paced while Sendra stood stiff with eternal patience. He came to her, ran a long finger across her neck, across a scar whitened by age. "It has become pretty on you, Sendra. There was a time when I found it repulsive, but now…"

Lukaan brushed aside tresses of blonde curls then buried his head into her neck, nibbling on the ridges of the scar. She flinched when he bit her. He lifted his head and let the caress fall down her shoulders, down her arms.

"We must change our plans. I need twenty of your best soldiers. Ones not afraid to die."

Sendra trembled under his touch. "The Gates of the Sun wait for all of us."

Lukaan wrapped his arms around her waist, his face pressed against her cheek. "We have time yet. Come with me. Later, we will discuss Antar."

ASSASSINS

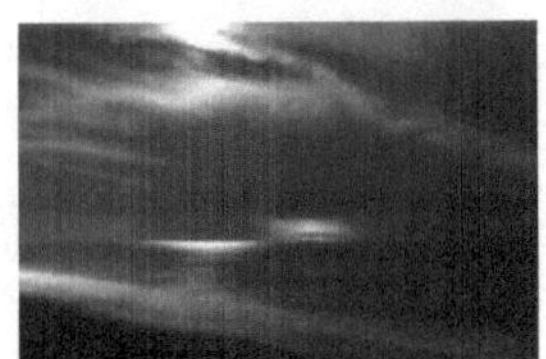

Savar, Fourth World in the Nelstar System
739 AD (After Darkness)
Second Cycle of the Third Moon
Second Calendar of Light

It was long after dusk when the messenger arrived at Manor du Savarra. Antar heard the announcement as he passed through the hallway. "Who is it, Benna?"

"A messenger, Master. He claims to have news regarding Lady Aentarra."

Long strides bore Antar to the entry with a few quick steps. He pushed past Benna. "Step in, soldier. What news do you bring of my daughter? Is she injured?"

"I'm with the Gore Canyon army, Lord Antar. We—"

"Aentarra is not at Gore Canyon."

"Yes, Lord Antar, I know, but we received news regarding her."

Antar noted the reddish brown dust on the man's uniform, a telltale sign of the canyon, and he could see the man was worn ragged from his trip. "Speak the news, soldier. And quickly."

"We captured a spy who said they had captured Aentarra. We know where she is."

Antar sent out a mind probe and tried to connect to her mind, but he found nothing. *Captive, then. They must be shielding her.* His heart raced while a storm raged in his mind. He felt the fires whirling in his eyes. *If they hurt her...*

"Take me to her. Now!"

The soldier cowed. "I cannot provide a direct shift point, Lord Antar, but I can get us close. We can walk the rest of the way."

"But, Master—"

"Not now, Benna." Antar nodded to the soldier while he infused himself with a shield. He seized the man's hand, retrieved the image from his mind, then Shifted. The Shift left a momentary void where they had been, and the slightest sound, as if a satin sheet had been ruffled.

Runella

Runella, Seventh World in the Nelstar System

"Take hold of each other first," Lukaan said, and stretched out his hands for the soldiers to grab. He formed an image in his mind from long ago, an image of a stone fireplace flanked by the heads of two giant boars, their tusks crossed like the swords of sentinels. When the focus was right, he Shifted. Two breaths later, he and seven soldiers stood in the parlor of Antar du Savarra's manor house.

Savar

Savar, Fourth World in the Nelstar System

In the kitchen, Molina busied herself helping with everything, no chore too menial for her, no challenge too much. Hair pushed back, face grimy, sleeves rolled to the elbow—Molina felt at ease.

In the midst of bandaging a leg wound on one of the cooks, she sensed a presence in the house. She stopped, quickly searching about until she found Benna. "Find someone to get a message to Antar. Quickly!" She then hurried toward the front of the house.

Molina swung open the double doors, gasping when she saw Lukaan. "What are you doing here? Get out!"

"You forget I was once an honored guest in the du Savarra house, Molina. Even Antar's shields can't keep me from Shifting here."

"He'll kill you for this. Something he should have done long ago."

"Perhaps long ago he could have. But don't worry, no harm will come to you. Not as long as Antar is reasonable." He nodded to the four soldiers on his left. "Grab hold of her. We need to leave."

"Don't you *dare* touch me." She said it to the soldiers, but her glare stayed fixed on Lukaan. When the soldiers moved closer, she shifted her gaze, freezing them. "I am Molina du Savarra. Do you *dare* to touch me?"

After a few seconds, Molina's gaze found Lukaan once again. "Why, Lukaan?"

For a moment, she thought sorrow touched his face, but then his steel gaze hardened.

"Antar must be stopped. The people are tired of the wars. They long for peace."

Her lips tightened and brown eyes narrowed. "The Council has sanctioned this?"

Lukaan nodded. "Antar must be stopped."

Molina leapt at him, her hand catching Lukaan on the side of the face. "It's *you* who must be stopped. Look at our beautiful city. Destroyed." Tears formed in her eyes. "So many dead."

She turned her back. "I'll hear nothing more of it. Do what you must with me, but I'll not have you speak ill of Antar."

"Don't worry, Molina. Once he swears the oath to stop the wars, you will be free to go."

She spun, head whipping back to face Lukaan. "But he would die if he breaks that oath."

"That is precisely the point." Lukaan nodded to the soldiers. "Let's go."

Molina thought quickly. "Wait. I must dress and get my jewelry. I can't go like this." She headed for the door.

Lukaan moved in front of her, checking the hall before he let her out.

"Stay alert, men. Twenty assassins won't keep Antar long. If he returns, you will wish the Goddess herself had eaten you." He led the soldiers up the stairs, checking every alcove before moving ahead, inspecting each shadow before passing it by.

Molina moved to the closet, carefully selecting clothes, then throwing them on the bed in a heap. Piled on top of a green dress, lay black shoes and an opal necklace. She pressed a button on the side of her dresser and the drawer of her nightstand slid open. She reached for a dagger that was laying atop a black velvet cloth.

They will not use me to kill Antar.

"No!" Lukaan dashed toward her.

Molina seized the dagger with both hands and plunged it into her heart. "I love you, Antar."

She screamed as the dagger pierced her flesh, then she collapsed.

Lukaan knelt beside her, his left arm supporting her head. He removed the dagger then cauterized the wound with fire, though he could tell he had been too late. Besides, he never was one for healing.

"May the gods help us all," one of the soldiers said. "What do we do now? He'll think we killed her. He'll blame us at the least."

Lukaan thought of what he needed to do. Vellana had warned him of the Council's fears. Now, he must deal with the consequences. "Clear off the bed, and—"

Lukaan felt the presence, so subtle, yet so distinct. In the time it took a heart to beat twice he analyzed the situation, dropped Molina on the bed then grabbed the soldiers nearest him. There was no time to take the others. He must leave before they fixed on his scent. An image formed of his own manor surrounded by guards. In the time it takes to blink an eye, he Shifted.

Once inside his house, Lukaan instructed the others. "Seek protection somewhere safe. I would suggest on Nagasha, but you be the one to decide. And hide well. Antar will be hunting for you."

~

From deep in the bowels of the manor, along secret passages known only to Antar, two Light Serpents shivered with vengeful lust. Antar had denied them the run of the manor when the storms had come—too many strange people in the house— and he had forgotten to issue an activation command when he left.

They could not fix the past, but they could seek revenge. The dark room hissed with light. With fire. The steel on the door heated. Turned red. Began to melt.

~

In an alley across the world, Antar and the soldier stepped through a rift onto a worn cobblestone street.

Ever alert, Antar's senses sprang to life: he heard feet scraping stone, cloth brushing against brick, smelled the tang of *menta* on nervous breaths. Racing hearts surrounded him, and the stench of fear-wrought sweat permeated the damp air.

Antar sensed all of this in an instant, even before the soldier accompanying him yanked his hand free.

Assassins peppered the alleys and buildings surrounding him, waiting like a nest of Bharan vipers. All were strong with the power but Antar had been weaving shields since before the Darkness—since before these pups had played with lighting candles from fingers of flame. It was going to take more than lightning or fire to infiltrate a shield of his.

cobblestone street

Lightning shot from a window behind him, a strike to the center of his back. *Blackfire* roared from the shadows. A barrage of fire and lightning poured forth from men lurking behind crates and hiding around bends and corners. It continued for some dozen moments, until the walls of the alley cracked and the cobblestone streets smoldered. Soon the smoke cleared, revealing that Antar's shield had absorbed the assaults.

He let them think for a moment, let them worry. "Count your heartbeats. You have five to decide. Whoever tells me about Aentarra will live to see the sun."

Antar struck the messenger first. It was only right; he was the worst of the betrayers.

A thin stream of fire shot from Antar's hand and bored into the man's head. He fell like an oak to the woodsman's axe. The building behind Antar erupted into flames, devouring the man who had cast the first assault. He screamed as he fell to the street from his perch at the window.

Antar's lightning targeted the man in the shadows of the alley ahead, piercing the shields of him and his cohort before striking them down. Burnt hair and seared flesh assaulted Antar's nostrils, but he stood firm. He located each of the remaining assailants then dispatched them with ruthless precision.

When the skirmish ended he counted twenty dead, twenty more wasted lives. The dead wore the symbol of the Red Sun, a designation of Lukaan's followers. It was a blazing red orb burned into their chest.

Antar dispatched a *slicer* to search for Aentarra—something he should have done before.

Curse Lukaan! Had he gone so far? Had She claimed so much of his soul that he resorted to assassins? Lukaan should have known they would never find me unprepared. It was a foolish...

Antar buckled. He felt a tear on his heart, like a limb being torn from his body. His chest hammered. "Molina!" His shout tore stones the size of men from the walls. And shook limbs from the trees.

Molina lay on the bed. Four soldiers gaped at the empty room, casting wary glances in all directions. They knew it wouldn't be long before Antar returned.

Eyes wide with fear, they moved toward the door. None of them could Shift. They would have to leave the manor on their own accord.

The lead soldier stopped, nose twitching like a dog on the hunt. "Do you smell that? Like burnt metal..."

The next moment, a flickering tongue pierced the door, its forked tip striking the air. Tasting, locking onto scents.

The soldier struck it with lightning, a direct hit on its venomous tongue. Seconds later, like a serpent breaching water, a black nose and face pushed through the thick door. It absorbed the soldier's lightning into its cavernous mouth, quenching its thirst.

"Light serpent!" one of the soldiers screamed before falling to the floor. Then he crawled to the corner and curled up to hide.

The second serpent entered through the ceiling, emerging from a tree in a fresco as if it had been lurking in the branches all along. Plates of black-on-black scales wrapped around a body as thick as a big man's leg. It slithered down a post of the bed, twisting along the carvings, then stretched out toward the soldier standing closest.

"Behind you!" the first man said. He summoned *blackfire* to smite the serpent. Eyes like diamonds on black velvet glowed, drawing the fire into them. Two other guards shot lightning. It flowed across the scales like moonlight on the crests of waves.

A hiss erupted from behind the soldiers. The sound crept through their pores, dragging fear with it. They turned to see the first serpent rising from the floor, swaying to a silent rhythmic beat. When one of them called fire to his hands, the serpent slid toward him, its cavernous maw baring curved fangs. A black ooze covered the soldier, immobilizing him, then the serpent turned toward the others.

The first man fell to his knees, pleading to a Goddess he had grown to fear, though now he feared these serpents even more. Her name was on his lips as the ooze flowed down his cheeks.

The second serpent wrapped its tail around a soldier, twisting and squeezing him until he looked like a maid's washcloth. Next it took the one cowering in the corner. The soldier had his head buried in his hands. He screamed when the tongue touched him.

The serpent incapacitated the soldier with a thin spreading of ooze, then dragged him to the center of the room to join the others. Fulgid black scales intertwined in a joyous celebration. Tongues flickered with each heartbeat, while diamond eyes glowed. It was time to feast.

~

It took only an instant for Antar to shift back to the manor. He expected the worst. "Molina!" his tone pleading as he took the stairs two and three at a time. He burst through the doors, tears already forming. The bed was bloodied, the smell of death fresh.

"What have they done to you?" Antar fell onto the bed, her body lay limp in his arms. She lay there like so many times before. This time, though, there would be no caressing, no soft kisses, no love to share. He grimaced at the blood staining her skin. Wept at the pain she must have suffered. "My dear, Molina. My love. What have I done?"

He kissed the seared scar on her chest, a low persistent keening, as if the dead sought their souls, rumbling through the room. Antar's tears rolled over her cheeks and mixed with her blood. He cursed every lost moment, every breath he should have shared with her. Large hands bulging with veins stroked her beautiful hair. He pulled her to his chest, rocking, caressing.

Moments later he felt the change coming. Muscles tightened. Tears dried. Soon his blood boiled, and though he tried to restrain himself, a bolt of *blacklightning* escaped the rage and tore through the floor, through the ground itself.

Antar stood, taking time to focus. He would need all of his concentration to track them. His powers converged at a point near the center of his mind, then spread through his body and into the room.

Within moments Antar sensed the presence. He knew at once it had been Lukaan. *So far he had fallen!* During the wars he had shown himself to be a pitiless and unremitting opponent, but even during the darkest days he would never have stooped so low.

And now he has done this to my Molina. To his own sister.

It had been a long time since a tear had stained Antar's cheek before today. The last time was during the birth of his beloved daughter, Aentarra, when he thought he might lose her *and* his wife.

Antar forced the emotions aside while he completed the search. All assassins leave trails, and if they left just a mote of dust caught in a flicker of starlight, he could track them. He soon identified the scent—the trail led to Nagasha.

So Lukaan did not act alone. No matter. Soon they will all be dead. Fools! Did they think I could forgive what they have done to Molina? Examples must be set. Molina must be avenged.

He felt the fires dancing in his head and fought to restore the calm before it went too far.

He staggered about the room then back to the bed, and sat. So many nights had he shared his love with Molina here: cool spring nights under satin sheets, summers with windows open praying for a breeze, and winters snuggled together under woolen blankets and heavy quilts. He recalled the children jumping and playing games, and pets who refused the hardwood floors to curl up at the bottom of the bed.

The two Light Serpents crept across the bed, silent as smoke. Forked tongues carried Antar's tears away. Diamond eyes sought approval. Antar stroked their heads, eliciting soft hisses and a writhing caress from each. "You should have left them alive. How I would have loved some time with them."

Louder hisses from angry nostrils defended their act. Cheek to cheek with him now, their sinuous movements soothed him. He stared into the diamond eyes, saw in the reflection that fire had replaced the tears in his own. "Yes, I know. But don't worry, there will be time for vengeance. There is *always* time for that. For now, though, things must be done my way. Go back. Maintain the vigil. Never again will I leave you unprepared."

Undulating in a downward spiral, the Light Serpents slithered off the bed and through the floor.

LIGHT OF LIGHTS

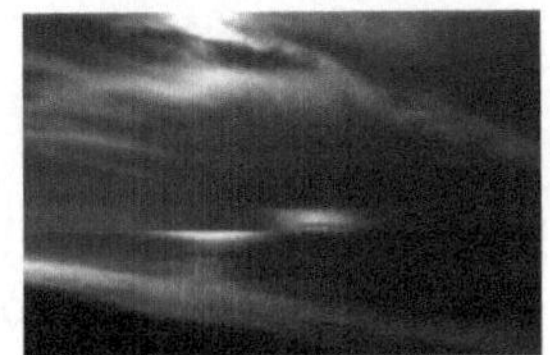

Savar, Fourth World in the Nelstar System
739 AD (After Darkness)
Fourth Cycle of the Third Moon
Second Calendar of Light

The moons had cycled twice since Molina had passed, and still Antar could not clear his mind. He had not exacted his vengeance yet, but a du Savarra could wait centuries for revenge. Besides, he knew now that Nagasha was in on the plot. And he knew they woke each morning expecting his counterstrike, went to bed each night wondering when it would come. Days on end filled with anxiety. Nights on end with little sleep. A strategy in itself.

Thinking about it took him away again. There were times when he wondered if he still had the heart for war, but those thoughts proved to be fleeting moments, for just as his undying love for Molina had not faded, neither had his thirst for blood been quenched.

Antar had already decided that his vengeance would not take the normal course. There would be no more destruction. No more devastation. There would have to be a peace arranged, one that would unify the worlds once more. With this in mind, Antar sent word to the other Lights via a mind link.

"Arrange a peace."

Yes, a peace. Let them believe that. They would have to believe it if they were to drop their natural defenses and leave their sick minds unprotected. Yes, the offer of peace should work fine. They must never think they can touch my family. I will show them what it means to incur the wrath of du Savarra vengeance.

Several days later a messenger arrived from the Hall bearing news for Antar's ears only. The other Lights had proposed a peace plan under the guise of a trial. They implied that this was a trap to catch Lukaan. Antar held no doubt it had been set to snare him instead. No matter. This would flush them out. He would see who stood on whose side. Then, he could act.

But first Nagasha.

I would end it all right now if not for Aentarra. I must ensure her safety. I promised Molina—

A sudden pain staggered him, knees crashing on hard plank flooring. Clenched fists helped him to concentrate as he strove to contend with the agony. Blood dropped from his forehead. More dribbled from his ear. Antar focused, tried to stop the rage in his mind.

Help me, Molina.

Crawling on all fours, he struggled to reach the bedpost, then pulled himself to his feet. A rivulet of blood sprouted from his temple. More fell from his ear, painting a crooked streak on his neck. He would need all of his power now. All of his wits. Another battle was coming, another struggle within.

Antar molded trembling hands into a vise that closed around his head. He shut his eyes, focused his power, then squeezed viciously in a struggle to reclaim command of his mind—the Others had seized control again.

The sieges had grown worse of late and, at times, their will seemed as strong as his own. But he had not risen to be the Light of Lights by nurturing a feeble mind. With a resolve tempered during a century of war, he quashed the insurrection.

He took a deep breath and closed his eyes. It was only one more day that he had control, but perhaps another day was all that he needed.

How long had it been? Aeons, it seemed, and yet this resistance had begun little more than a hundred years past, shortly after the onset of the Wars of Light. Now the attacks had grown worse, and the Others were growing stronger.

A voice from the corridor interrupted his reflection. "Good morning, Master. The *keetah* birds have sung another fine day; it bodes well for the trial."

Antar smiled at the old superstition. "Lay out my best outfit, Benna. The Council of Light will deliver the verdict today. I intend to look the part."

The old servant smiled. "You would look regal even in rags, My Lord." The smile stayed with him as he limped toward the back of the closet, fingering each garment as he passed. He could no longer see the colors, but he knew where each one hung on the rack and he knew their touch, each as distinct as the bones on a man's face.

Benna was meticulous about selecting the outfit: silk trousers dark as ebony, a high-collar ivory shirt, and midnight–blue armbands. It was not the most elegant outfit in the wardrobe, but after two centuries of service Benna knew what brought out the best in his master.

He laid the clothes on the bed and smoothed each pleat and wrinkle. The bed was huge, almost chest-high on Benna. It was wide enough to accommodate six or eight in comfort, and yet, since Antar's wife had died the satin quilts had not been mussed even once.

Benna knew his master had slept little of late, and when he did it was the back of his favorite chair that cushioned his head.

Old skin stretched as the servant reached to the top of the closet and removed the Crimson Victory Cape. It was almost as old as Antar and as thick and pure as the blood in his veins. It was even rumored that the dye used to stain the cape contained the blood of Antar's enemies.

Benna sighed and shook his head as he laid the cape open on the bed. "The Light of Lights being tried like a commoner. It is a sin against the Blood."

"There are many sins these days, my friend."

Antar seemed to have startled the old servant. "I'm sorry, Master. I didn't hear you. I'm afraid age has dulled my senses."

"None of us have the ears of a fox anymore." Antar stopped to examine the wardrobe. "You must favor that wardrobe selection, Benna. You choose it for every important occasion."

"It honors you, Master, and gives you strength. Today they will fear you. Enough to—"

"Enough to acquit me? I think not. This is not about guilt or innocence; this is for show." Antar's smile held a suspicious twist. "But soon enough they will fear me. And they will pay for their treachery."

"What about the trial? Why are you going?"

Antar stared at a portrait of Molina hanging on the wall, Aentarra by her side, long hair brushing her back, and her twisted smile lighting the room. "I will do what is necessary to ensure her safety. I suspect the trial is a trap…but sometimes hunters get fooled."

Benna's brow furrowed. "If Lukaan has the support of the other Lights…"

"I'll take care of Lukaan. As to the others… they'll have to bare their teeth. And when they do…"

"Do you think they will banish you, Master?"

Laughter filled the room. "We are far beyond banishment, my friend. But don't worry, I'll take care of you." Antar patted Benna's back, then once again became lost in the portrait.

Benna moved to the nightstand, where he straightened a few books and dusted the lamp. The shuffle of his feet on the floor brought Antar back to the conversation.

"Besides, Benna, the wars will end soon."

"Will they, Master? When? We have not surrendered, have we?"

Antar's glare cut through the old man's near-blindness. "Surrender? Never! But the wars *will* end, Benna."

Antar moved to the reflector to finish dressing, completing a mental review of the calculations as he did. *Now*, he thought, then closed his eyes and issued the directive to the *slicers*. Soon they would be traveling to Nagasha, the cowardly city that harbored the assassins who had killed his wife.

For the third time in as many moons the smile was forced from his face, a smile that had seemed perpetual, even during the darkest days of the war.

"Molina..." Her name slipped past his lips for the thousandth time in so few days—so few days that had worn on him like centuries. He could almost feel the indelible scars that marred his soul, each one a dagger in his heart.

He filled his lungs with several deep breaths, brushed back a few loose strands of hair and stared into the mirrored glass. The once coalblack hair had faded now, giving way to streaks of gray on the sides, but it induced no worry; the gray had been a companion since the beginning of the wars, a gentle reminder that even he, the Light of Lights, grew older given enough time.

Antar's gaze hardened into a glare that would make the strongest men cringe. How dare they put him to the trial, like some merchant caught with a false set of weights. Black flames flickered in Antar's eyes, threatening the onset of another convulsion, though he fought the impulse and regained control.

Benna tapped Antar's shoulder. "Master, are you all right?"

Antar shook his head, but then nodded. "I'm fine." He took time to focus. He must maintain composure, at least until this was over.

Although his own fate was about to be determined, it was not his fate alone, and Antar was willing to suffer unspeakable horrors as long as he stopped Lukaan. What did he have left after Molina?

Aentarra. How could he forget the most precious of all his daughters, even while wallowing in misery?

To lose her would be to truly lose life. More.

A reluctant smile lit his eyes, and the brush in his hand touched lightly on an elegant tinge of silver, a single errant strand that he cajoled into place before letting the brush settle to the dressing table.

As soon as Antar backed away from the reflector, Benna limped to the bureau holding his master's most prized possessions: *ergond* boots, a *seglar* sash, and the *faela* necklace. Few others owned even one of them; no one but Antar owned all three.

It had taken Antar six full moons to capture the *ergonds* he wanted, a pair of majestic black specimens with no spots, but his diligence was duly rewarded. Once an *ergond* was captured and placed in service, it served its master with uncompromising loyalty, and though *ergonds* were most often used for gloves or caps, Antar swore there was nothing to match the sensation of wearing living boots. Parchment thin and more resilient than leather, they moderated temperature for comfort.

Antar wrapped the *seglar* sash around his slim waist. Each time he put it on, it spurred memories of the first time he wore it. He and Molina had hosted a ball for the elite of Nelstar, and even though all the women had expressed their admiration for Molina's gown, their secret envy was for Antar's sash. The sash was darker than midnight, but the *seglar* worms had spun pulsing lights into it, so that the sash sparkled like the stars.

From a silver tray atop the bureau, Benna lifted the *faela* necklace from a tray of liquid where they fed. He fastened it around his master's neck. The necklace itself consisted of a colony of *faela*, acting as one organism, one mind. The smile stretched Antar's cheeks wide as he recalled the agony of the gathering. The search for the *faela* had taken Antar to their spawning site, deep in rock crevices among the roots of giant trees that sprang from the Lake of the Dead. They were captivating creatures that altered shape and color to complement whatever object they adorned.

In his final act of self-adornment, Antar slipped the Warrior Ring of Nelstar on his right index finger. He already wore on his left hand the Ring of Light, reserved for the Light of Lights, the Seventh One, the Eternal Flame.

The dazzling beams from the Ring of Light clashed with the brilliant emerald rays of the Warrior Ring whenever their trajectories crossed. The two rings should never have been worn by the same person. Lights were forbidden to engage in battle—their power too destructive—yet Antar had done more than just participate; he had been the catalyst for it all.

As he turned to leave, the beams from the rings struggled for dominance, each blinding ray crashing into the other as he moved.

When Antar and Benna reached the main hall, they found the other servants lined up like guards awaiting inspection, but with their heads bowed, both in respect and as protection against the light. It proved to be a wise precaution, for today the aureole was forbidding; even Benna shielded his failing eyes from the brilliant light.

"You have been faithful, my friends, and your allegiance shall be rewarded." A pouch appeared in Antar's palm, a sleight of hand that no magician could have performed better. Antar handed the pouch to Benna.

"Inside is the key to my coin room, where you will find a green chest marked with the seal of du Savarra. Divide the coins in the chest among yourself and the other servants according to length of service."

"My Lord is most gracious, but we do not deserve such a reward."

Antar shook his head. "Some people favor kindness near the end, Benna, as if it will somehow restore their youth or pardon past sins, but that is not my motivation. And I harbor no illusions about my life, nor do I have regrets. The setting sun has been as kind as the dawn."

He pulled Benna to him in a tight embrace, hugged him. "There is a second chest in the coin room. It is marked with your own seal—"

"Master, I have no seal, I am but a—"

"You have a seal now, old friend. And you have a manor south of Lake Mago."

Tears formed in Benna's eyes as Antar continued.

"There is enough gold in the chest to last your life and more. I would have done this earlier, but... I was selfish, wishing more for your company than your happiness."

Benna wiped tears from his eyes with both sleeves. "This is all moot, My Lord. I will be serving you for many more seasons."

"It is time for me to go, Benna."

The old servant moved spryly for his age, hurrying toward the massive front door carved from one of the giant sentinel trees that he and Antar had planted when he first entered his employ. "Masuto, the carriage," Benna called. "And hurry, our master is ready."

"I need no carriage today. I want the people to see me and to remember the destiny they have written for themselves. The Council said the people insisted on a trial. Let them have one. Let them see what they have wrought."

"But, Master, there are those who might try to harm you."

"I know, Benna. I want them to be standing among the crowds. I would like to see their faces as I stroll the Way. See their glares. Hear their taunts. I hope they find courage to show themselves. It will make for a stimulating walk."

Antar fastened the clasp on his cape. He noted a glittering reflection from the steel of an ancient sword affixed to a shield on the wall. A helmet inscribed with markings few could read was suspended above the sword, and two of the finest daggers he had ever seen flanked it. He had long ago abandoned the use of steel as a weapon, but it served as a steadfast reminder of a vanished era. Steel would be no more effective than throwing stones in the civilization where Antar stood trial.

A pair of servants swung open the massive front doors that guarded the entrance, doors that stretched a full span high and were adorned with the heads of wild boars, their tusks still ivory–white and as sharp as when they had been alive. Some in the city claimed that the boars yet lived, that their fierce snorts could be heard at night.

Antar glided down the stairs, the Crimson Victory Cape fluttering in the breeze he created, and the *seglar* sash sparkling like the desert sky on a moonless night in Ambris. If he lacked a natural bounce today, the *ergonds* that were his boots provided it, and the *faela* that constituted his necklace danced in a macabre rhythm to the blinding beams from his rings.

The Way was lined a hundred deep on each side, soldiers stiff with duty standing sword-to-sword to guard the path and keep it clear of debris. As Antar stepped forward, the *ergond* boots sought purchase on the slippery cobblestone street, while the *faela* necklace trapped beams of light from the sun and sprayed them over his Crimson Cape. All the while, the *seglar* sash's pulsing lights announced to everyone who was coming. There could be no doubt.

Antar scanned the crowd and caught sight of many that he recognized: millers and carpenters who had worked on his house, the butcher from whom Benna bought the meat, and the candle maker with his family of six.

Small children rode on their fathers' shoulders and orphans crowded between the legs of beggars, merchants, and even prostitutes, for the chance to get a glimpse of the Light of Lights. For the most part, these were common people with hope in their hearts but fear in their minds —poor souls hoping to steal a glimpse of Antar du Savarra, to see the Light and be bathed in the grace of his glory.

Antar did not intend to disappoint them. He let go the shield that encompassed his nimbus, unleashing the full brilliance of his aura.

A bystander screamed as if struck by a weapon. "I'm blind!"

Many averted their heads, while rabid believers opened their eyes and stared straight ahead. Soon the shrieks of pain caused by burnt retinas spread along the Way. They could no more stare at the sun than at Antar du Savarra unsheathed.

Now onlookers crowded the guards on the streets, but they did so with their eyes closed, pushing hands, arms, and legs through any crack available to try to steal a touch of his light.

"I'm healed!" a woman shouted, and somewhere to the left a man proclaimed the miraculous cure of his legs.

Guards hid their eyes while trying to keep the crowd at bay. And so the walk along the Way went. Some people cursed him as the heir to the Goddess herself, an ages–old legend of suffering and death that only the eldest of Nelstar remembered, but even the faintest hint of remembrance was enough to terrify men.

Others along the Way heralded him as the savior, the one destined to stop the endless wars and bring peace to all the lands. "Save us, Antar. Bring us peace."

The emotions of the mob swayed with the prevailing wind. It wasn't long before this crowd echoed the newest call, clamoring for him to be their savior. "Bring us peace, Antar. End the war."

The smile remained on Antar's face even as he approached the Hall of Light.

Fools. Have they forgotten that they blamed me for starting the war?

The closer he drew to the Hall of Lights, the more hostile the crowd became, currying favors from the other Lights. People always sought the ones who held power, and those that showered curses on him now did so sensing a change, anticipating the outcome of the trial—but only when they thought his head was turned, when he could not see who had forsaken him.

Antar smiled at their petty deceptions. He would let them revel in the moment. He felt certain that his time would come again.

The chamber inside shook with the reverberations while, outside, throngs of people crowded the square and jammed the streets, pushing and shoving to get near him, like maggots swarming a carcass, and all screaming his name. Some pleaded to the Lights to have mercy on him, others sought mercy from him, but the majority shouted for blood and cursed his vile existence. The common ground was that all held his name on their lips, and with their shouts the chamber trembled. "Antar! Antar!"

Antar heard the maledictions and the denunciations. He saw the deceit in their eyes. The raspy caw of the tanner's wife caught his ear, a woman who had felt no compunction about taking his coin when her child fell ill, and she needed a healer brought in from two worlds away. Now, she condemned him.

Cowering behind a sniveling dowager he saw the unmistakable form of Pallo Jorn, his rotund shape too big to conceal behind the woman's frail frame.

As well to try to hide a cow behind a cat.

Antar recognized his shape, as well as his voice, and he remembered when Pallo had fawned and bootlicked just to get near him, to be seen in his presence.

But worst of all, he heard the mocking clucks of those who had once called him kin, and those who had sought his beneficence and business acumen when their own fortunes had languished. But even through that he smiled.

They cannot take away the time I have already lived. They cannot touch the memories or the glory.

The entrance to the hall loomed ahead, the steps lined with fountains gushing streams of water reputed to have miraculous healing properties. Ironic, that the soothing sound of water would greet Antar on this, of all days, when he had paid it no mind for so long. It was Molina who had always noticed the little things, one of the many reasons why he loved her so much—she never let the joys of life slip by her.

Antar's chest heaved with a heavy breath. A thousand awaited him at the steps leading to the chamber, one thousand of the strongest guards. He recognized Valrye and Therram, two of the strongest shield—weavers, and knew the Lights had chosen well. Antar's smile lifted his cheeks high.

Their fear is strong today. I can feel it.

He could already see the shields forming, the youngest guards as tentative as boys on their first boar hunt, but the others, if not confi-dent, were steady, and their weaving was strong. He knew that once he started the ascent the shields would entomb him, air enough to breathe, no more.

Antar paused, turned, and looked back along the Way toward his palace, where the doors were now closed. Some in the crowd must have thought he was taking a last look at his realm—others that he hesitated because he was reluctant to face judgment. Little did anyone know that Antar had been counting time during his proud walk to the Hall, and that even now, as he arrived at the steps to the Hall of Lights, the *slicers* were on the outskirts of Nagasha awaiting his final command.

JUDGMENT

Nagassa, First World in the Nelstar System
739 AD (After Darkness)
Fourth Cycle of the Third Moon
Second Calendar of Light

*A*ntar searched his mind for the vision, seeking the optimum site for observation. *There*, he thought, and ordered the *slicer* to a vantage point high above the city.

~

Lurking in the ever–present fog outside of Nagasha, the *slicers* hovered in the dense areas close to the ground and in the misty tendrils that wrapped around trees and shrubs.

Slicers were thinner than one of Antar's gray hairs. A small branch could conceal hundreds, a tree trunk many thousands. They sat motionless—a massive army poised to strike, pulsing with power, their shimmering light dimmed in preparation for the assault.

Inside the city gates, unsuspecting citizens prepared for another day:

loaves of bread rose in the bakers' shops, babies cried for their mother's milk, and the morning-watch had arrived to relieve tired guards of their late–night duty. In the distance, a slight glint of light reflected off the *slicers* as the first rays of sunlight burned through the fog.

~

Across several worlds and the void of space, Antar du Savarra stood outside the Hall of Lights staring into an empty sky. With not so much as a nod, or even a blink of the eye, he issued the final directive.

~

They erupted from their hidden positions, sparking a luminescence that collided with the morning rays and shone like mirrored glass on a summer day in the Bhara.

A loaf of potato bread and a serving of khaffe had been the baker's first order of the day. He never collected his coppers—two *slicers* burst into the shop and struck the soldiers who had been his customers. They took a few last breaths before collapsing to the floor.

Three streets away, a mother with four children in tow struggled with the steep incline to her master's estate. As they achieved the crest of the hill they discovered five *slicers* had dispatched the guards at the gate. The children never cried though, and fear stayed their mother's tears. Soon, even those who caroused all night and kept a late bed were jarred from slumber by cries of death.

Slicers screamed through streets and penetrated walls, fortresses proved to be as vulnerable as a cutpurse's shed. Nowhere was safe, and those whose lives were spared could only wonder why.

Not a single guard from the night-watch made it home. The morning relief lay in a crumpled heap at the gates to the palace. Frightened horses stormed through the streets, riders stripped from their saddles.

Carts laden with valuables sat unguarded. And all the while fruit merchants, peddlers, and other vendors remained unscathed.

The blacksmith dropped his bellows as if it were as hot as his fire and raced home. The whimpering of the dog told the tale. He turned the corner to find the dog licking his son's lifeless face—a new recruit in the guard. He found his wife and daughter on the kitchen floor shivering. He had just enough time to shed a stream of tears before a *slicer* delivered him to his son.

The city pulsed with light reflecting off the *slicers*. The air shuddered. Sounds of death permeated the city: a humming *slicer* cut short the final curse from a thief in the midst of counting loot, and the swish of a crystal shard silenced a priest's last prayer at the altar to the Goddess.

On a corner in the merchants' district an entire crowd succumbed when a mass of shivering light struck them. The brave made company with the cowards in seeking refuge, but no abode offered safety; the *slicers* found them all. They found the captain of the guard in his closet, and a jeweler with his assistant cowering in a hidden cellar. They found fathers under beds with small children hidden beneath them, but those they left alone. They sought out every breath, no matter how small, and every heartbeat, no matter how faint, delivering judgment with severe discrimination.

Through it all the assassins remained unharmed, though the spectacle of death drove them to seek safety at the manor of their benefactor.

Soon the city was quiet, save for the lamenting of survivors, the whines of pets, and the terrified whickering of riderless mounts. East of the city, inside a manor owned by one of the Lights, the assassins babbled and waited for death.

"He's here! I knew this would happen. The man is mad."

One lone assassin stood to face his fate. "Do you think anyone will protect us now? Not likely. Not Lukaan. Not even Her."

The room fell silent as *slicers* appeared, specters of death hovering in midair. They struck one–by–one, though death was not instant. The *slicers* inflicted each assassin with the pain most unbearable to them.

One felt the flames sting his feet then engulf his body until he begged for death with each breath. Another assassin tried to run but experienced the pain of bones shattering in his legs. He felt the snap of each bone and the jab of each splinter through muscle.

The last of them cried in anticipation of his own fate, but only when he realized how he would die did he weep—when he found himself immobile, trapped in a narrow rock passage with nowhere to go and no air to breathe. And even then the horror did not register until he gasped when he tried to take breath.

After the last of the assassins expired, the *slicers* sought the others in the manor, including the lady and her son, the last of Nagasha's citizens destined to fall.

Savar, Fourth World of the Nelstar System

Savar night sky

Antar turned to face the guards awaiting him on the steps to the Hall of Lights. Their muscles tensed, eyelids flickered. Some of the younger ones twitched with fear. A hint of a smile crossed Antar' face.

They are afraid, he thought, and stepped into their web.

The massive doors sealed shut behind Antar, extinguishing the noise of the crowd. He waited outside the main chamber for a signal of how to proceed. A Seal of Silence fused the doors and formed a solid grid over the walls and windows. It would soon be impenetrable.

~

The chamber was constructed like the arena, with three broad bands of seats to keep the social classes separated. A full span above the highest band of seats, a circular platform hovered with no visible means of structural support save a twisting set of stairs. Around a table on the platform sat five of the Lights.

Vellana stood to address the other Lights. Chandra might be the oldest but that did not guarantee she would be the successor. Rings of light-brown curls dangled in front of each ear, appearing darker against Vellana's pale skin.

"We must wait until Valrye assures us that Antar is secure. Only then do we risk bringing him in."

Her lavender robe did nothing to disguise her voluptuous body. A few of the Lights knew that figure better than her husband; still, they could not help but watch her every move.

Bolledar's thick fingers gripped white linen and dabbed beads of sweat from his forehead. "There is no need to continue the trial. Kill him as soon as the shield is complete."

Vellana spoke to his suggestion while appearing to ignore him. "He must have a formal trial, or at least what appears to be a formal trial to the people. The people support us now, but if we suffer setbacks in the absence of Antar's leadership they might just as quickly turn against us."

"What we can't risk is a trial," Bolledar said, his labored breath parting puffy lips. "If we give him a trial, the punishment is set in stone; we can banish him at worst, and I have no intention of keeping guards at my back for eternity. Everyone knows how those du Savarras are about vengeance." His hands shook as he loosened his collar.

Vellana raised her hand to strike him, but managed to stay the attack. "Who will slay the giant? You, Bolledar?"

"Together we can."

"For us to kill him we must release the shield. Then he will know our intentions. Do you know what the wild boar does when cornered?" She let the pause still Bolledar.

"Yes, I believe you do. Even the worst of hunters knows it is not wise to corner a wild boar. And there are more than a few reasons why Antar chose that particular beast for his symbol. Besides, we can dispose of Antar once he is in exile. There are more ways than one to cut his tusks. He has three daughters."

Chandra stood, her gaze finding Vellana. "We have more of a dilemma than you realize. Don't be foolish enough to think he is here for a trial. I'm convinced Antar knows."

Chandra looked at each of them. "Yes, he knows. And I'm certain he is here to kill us. We must be prepared to do anything to stop him. If forced into it, we could use the Book."

"Never!" Bolledar leapt to the challenge on shaky legs.

Vellana had not expected Chandra to be so bold. *Is she trying to make a play for the Seat?* "The Book is dangerous. It has not been used since—"

"Since the Darkness." Chandra did not shy from the word like the others. "Antar used it, and he eluded death's song. Lukaan has also felt the touch of the Book."

The lavender robe clung to Vellana as she moved around the table. She must do something to stifle Chandra. "Yes, Antar used it. But look at him. The howls of more than wolves haunt his manor. I have even heard he keeps Light Serpents—if you believe they exist. He is as mad as the moon, and *I* believe the Book is responsible."

Vellana paused, checking to see that Lukaan was secure behind his shield. When she saw that he was, she continued with a whisper. "And as to Lukaan, I believe a close examination of him supports my theory. He is closer to madness than he is reality; however, he is the only one strong enough to help us with Antar, so his is a problem we will be forced to accept. For now."

Chandra's smile faded to a frown. "Tell me, Vellana. What were you doing at Antar's manor?"

"You flatter me, Chandra, but for no good cause. Antar had his Molina, and he was forever faithful."

Vellana let her gaze roll around the table, noting the looks from the others. "We are not here to discuss morality, fellow Lights. Let us proceed."

The five Lights met Antar in the antechamber, a room as large as most buildings. Tapestries from before the Darkness adorned the walls, and ancient weapons stood as reminders of eras long since gone.

With not so much as a nod to acknowledge Antar's presence, they inspected the shield, the furrows on their brows not relaxed until they were comfortable with his impotence. The guards had been meticulous in weaving the shield. No thread was out of place.

Chandra lingered after the other Lights had gone. The ages had been kind to her. Her dark-brown skin was still smooth, save a large burn on her right forearm, and she had a light pigmentation on the left cheek in the shape of a half moon. She suffered the burn at the Battle of Katsintal, during the wars, and she had never forgiven Antar for the wound.

"Therram, we will prepare the way. Keep him secure until we call." Chandra frowned, her eyes focusing on Antar. Frowns came easy after centuries of scowling. She leaned toward the shield and looked at Antar before leaving. "Today we will expunge that smile from your face, Light of Lights."

Antar glowered. "Release your dogs, Chandra. We will settle the matter without the formalities of a trial. And this time there will be no need for subterfuge. You and the others can openly join forces with Lukaan." Antar's smile was disarming. "Did you ever think to fool me anyway?"

The icy glare touched Chandra with fear. She knew that Antar would relish an engagement right here in the Sacred Hall. Nothing would gratify him more than to perpetuate the wars. *The man is truly mad,* Chandra thought, and gave Antar her back.

"We will come for him soon, Therram." Chandra's suspicious eyes scoured the hall before her whisper caught Therram's ear. "Kill anyone who approaches."

T he five Lights re-entered the main hall and, in unison, five seats slid from the table to accommodate them. After each took a seat—and once the crowd settled down—Chandra rose to deliver his address.

Heads in the room nodded acknowledgment with each statement.

"The Light of Lights has erred. The Shining One has sinned. Hereafter, let Antar du Savarra's name be imbued in your memories, but not as the Light of Lights, not as the Eternal Flame, and not as He Who Drank the Darkness; instead, let him be remembered by what he brought upon himself—Antar du Savarra, 'The Light That Failed.'"

The muttering grew among the onlookers, even among the one hundred who awaited trial, the highest ranking officers from both factions during the Wars of Light. Of those on the lowest level, even Antar's enemies must have held some degree of compassion for him—for a man who had risen so high then fallen so far.

But one set of eyes showed neither compassion nor fear. Held behind a shield similar to Antar's, Lukaan's eyes burned red with the fires of retribution.

Chandra continued to strut about the platform, admonishing the Light of Lights. "He has shattered your trust and flaunted his power. Lights are forbidden from the art of war, and yet he brandished his considerable talents for more than a century. Deaths are still being recorded. For that he should pay."

Chandra sensed the growing acceptance to the Lights' way of thinking. The tides were moving in their direction. "But for his other crimes, for taking husbands from their wives and fathers from their children—for these atrocities he *must* pay. The Book of Books demands it. It *must* be done.

"The hills and valleys echo with shouts for justice, and along the boulevards, walking the streets, and hiding in the back alleys of every city, people of all ranks call for a reckoning. Even in his own city, outside his own door, the people whisper prayers for peace."

Chandra scanned the room for dissenters, calculating who was with them and who was not, then she turned toward the antechamber where Antar was held. "We tire of the war, Light of Lights. When will you stop persecuting your people? When will you bring us peace?"

Chandra heard the murmurs of approbation that urged her on, support that the Lights felt was crucial to sanction the process. Her voice resounded throughout the chamber. "Bring him in, Therram."

One thousand of the strongest had linked together, their shields woven with the secrecy of the ages, and though the ward held Antar at bay, it could not contain his resplendence—the chamber was suffused with blinding light, as if the sun itself paid visit. Everyone knew who entered—the Light of Lights, the Eternal Flame, The Seventh One, He Who Drank the Darkness.

And even now, with him trapped behind a shield held by a thousand of the council guard, Antar sensed that many in the room dreaded the decision to cast their support to the other Lights, fearing the retribution it might bring.

Chandra Matha, eldest of the Lights, held the floor. Antar knew Chandra had always envied him the High Seat. For many years it rubbed her like an itch that refused to go away.

"Before we begin, Antar, we grant you the opportunity to redeem your honor. Confess your crimes, provide the information we require and then, if you plead convincingly enough, your punishment shall be alleviated."

Three short blasts from a herald's trumpet interrupted them, announcing the arrival of a messenger. As the doors opened to allow him access, the deafening roar of the mob in the square stole in with him. Guards escorted him to the landing, where the Lights questioned him in secret, after which they bade him take leave. It did not escape Antar's notice that shock painted each Light's face.

Chandra trembled. She waited until the doors had been shut and sealed following the messenger's exit, then her gaze swept the council guard holding Antar captive. A nod from Valrye brought Bolledar and Vellana. They joined Chandra at the edge of the platform.

Vellana signaled to the guards to bring Lukaan. "We might have need of his power."

Antar heard the gasp from the lower level of the chamber, where the hundred stood shoulder-to-shoulder. Lukaan was Antar's staunchest enemy, his antagonist during the wars. Only days past many of these one hundred had faced each other on the battlefield. Antar sensed the air, bristling with the impending threat of war.

Wary glances and glares bombarded the dais, where Chandra looked down upon Antar, her smile forced and thin. She waited until the guards brought Lukaan to the platform, then she and Bolledar descended to the landing where Antar stood.

"Where are they, Antar? Where have you hidden them?"

"Fools. Do you still believe I would let you put Lukaan in my place? Do you truly believe I would let him poison my people?"

Lightning streaked inside the shield, and fire tested its mettle. The *ergonds* shrieked and the *faela* necklace convulsed. Within heartbeats Antar calmed himself. "I hide nothing."

There was always a whisper of arrogance in Antar's voice. Today it was much more than a whisper.

Chandra cast a stolen glance at her brethren.

"Begging for concurrence, Chandra?"

"The *slicers*, Antar. Where are they?"

Silence marked the Light of Lights. Silence and a smile that unnerved Chandra.

"Nagasha was attacked this morning, Antar. This morning! After the peace had been arranged."

Antar let the accusation float in the air, his response a malevolent glare.

Chandra struggled to hold Antar's gaze, fists and jaw clenched before she succumbed. She darted her gaze from one end of the chamber to the other. "Why so confident, Antar? You must realize the position you are in. Or has madness succeeded in luring you to the other side?"

The remaining Lights stood to support Chandra, but it was Bolledar who found the words first. "You have not answered Chandra's question, Light of Lights. And we *do* require a response."

The light from Antar's eyes riveted Bolledar, like a cobra does a sparrow. "As you know me so well, fellow Light, you are aware that I do not respond to allegations made in the throes of anger; besides, I sanctioned no peace as yet. The Seal of du Savarra does not mark that accord."

Bolledar's face burned red. "This is a simple query, Antar. What knowledge have you of the attack? What role did you play in it?"

Antar's smile could be more chilling than his glare. Bolledar must have found it so today. "Why do you ask? Did you leave your family in Nagasha? Bera was not among them, was she?"

Bolledar's jaw tightened. "Respond to the questions."

"Were you aware that my wife was also slain? It hurts to lose someone you have spent an eternity with. I pray you did not suffer a similar fate."

Bolledar glowed. He seemed on the verge of an attack, but he managed to funnel the anger to his voice instead. "Did you do it, Antar? Did you kill Bera?"

Chandra stepped beside him, a calming touch meant to restrain Bolledar, though Bolledar brushed it aside with a swipe. "Did you kill her?"

Antar's eyes had not blinked since the questioning began. Pools of liquid fire were cooler, but as he glared at Bolledar, a tear escaped. "Did you know that I discovered who killed my Molina?"

Antar awaited no response. "Yes, Bolledar, I *know*. And I discovered the assassins' lair as well. Did you know that they found refuge in Nagasha? If I remember, you wield quite some influence in Nagashan politics."

Antar's glare was crippling, even through the tears that welled in his eyes and stained his cheeks. "You should have kept the killing to the warriors. You should have left my Molina alone."

Bolledar's skin poured sweat, and he looked as if he would collapse from the strain. "You killed two million people just to avenge your wife's death!" Most in the chamber shrank back upon hearing the numbers. Cries of anguish from those who had family or friends stirred the crowd, and soon, cries of retribution erupted from all levels of the chamber.

Antar knew that nothing short of death would appease them now, not after learning about Nagasha. "Yes, Bolledar, I killed them. No children, no innocents, only soldiers and those whose minds were already lost to Lukaan—including that shrew you called a wife and the coward you named a son. I would have killed ten times as many to avenge Molina."

A gasp rumbled through the chamber, even the other Lights shrank back. Only Antar's face remained expressionless.

Chandra advanced toward Antar, her blood was boiling and her voice was raised. "The *slicers*, Antar, where are they? We must know now, or—"

Chandra and Bolledar shriveled under the ferocity of Antar's glare, and the other Lights, though they held firm, seemed reluctant to move. The shield itself trembled at the force of his voice. "You want to know where the *slicers* are, Chandra. Very well, I shall show you."

Antar's arms drooped at his sides. His body slumped. If it had not been for the fire streaking the whites of his eyes, he might have appeared at rest. It was then that Antar called them. From somewhere in the distance they heard the summons.

SOUL TAKERS

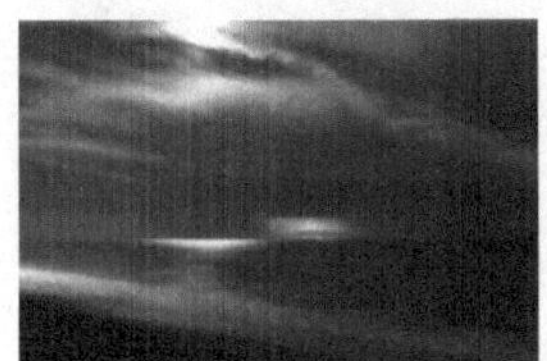

Therram sniffed the air, his senses on alert. He must have sensed the palpitations, the disturbance. He and Valrye examined the shield while other guards cast wary glances in all directions. "Stay the course, men. Something's astir."

The air grew still, deathly still, as if life had ceased to exist in the chamber. It bristled with heat. From the arena floor to the vaulted ceiling people gasped with each breath. The next moment icy vapors spewed from their mouths and they shivered with cold.

"I don't like this," Valrye shouted, his eyes darting to the windows and doors, hands cupped and ready to shoot flame.

The stained glass in the windows vibrated and rattled, then seemed to come alive as hundreds of projectiles breached the shields.

Domed ceiling of the Great Hall

Through it all not a splinter of glass fell to the floor, as if the windows allowed them entry.

From all directions they came, slender slivers of crystal-like substance that glowed with the force of the sun and traveled as fast as its light.

"Shards of Death," one guard screamed. Gasps of fear echoed their other names:

"Life-takers!"

"Soul-catchers!"

"*Slicers!*" Chandra yelled the warning. "Shield your minds."

Chaos ruled in the arena as the glimmering strands erupted from the marble floor that capped a mountain of rock. Hundreds more infiltrated the walls, a mass of stone that had withstood the forces of ages, had been deemed impregnable for thousands of years, and had even held during the Darkness Wars.

The slivers of death plunged through the roof. The holes they made sealed behind them. Not even light could get through. The tiny threads of death, or whatever Antar willed them to be, infused the air with their vibrations until the chamber shuddered as the sea does before a Gorshan Storm.

Many thousands answered the call, silently screaming across the chamber seeking predestined marks, piercing the guards' shields then their skulls.

They succumbed to the assault as lambs to a pack of wolves. As the guards fell, Antar saw that perhaps it would not be quick enough. The other Lights scrambled for the Book, and he could not yet escape the shield; too many guards clung to it even in the throes of death.

Antar glared across the room at Lukaan, waiting for the shields to drop, waiting to do battle.

When he sensed it might be over, he scanned the lower chamber for Aentarra then issued the order. A lone *slicer* hurtled toward her, weaving through the mob on bands of light with an image implanted from Antar: raven hair and thin lips—like Molina; her nose, too; her father's dark eyes but with pale skin; and a smile as infectious as baby's laughter.

She would only feel a pinprick before hearing his voice. "Take my thoughts, daughter, and my love. Never tell them where the *slicers* are hidden. And above all else, avenge me!"

A tinge of excitement coursed his veins when he felt the shield weakening, but even as his hopes were rekindled, he heard Chandra's panicked shout.

"Open the Book before he is free." The oldest of the Lights was not so calm now. He lunged for the Book. The other Lights hesitated.

"I know the Book is an unknown," Chandra said, "but Antar's vengeance is imminent. If we don't stop him now we'll die as surely as the millions on Nagasha."

Antar had prepared his own attack to coincide with the release of the shield, but he had not counted on them going for the Book, at least not this soon. He needed more time, just a little more, but they were too close.

Forced to alter his plans, he set a new course of action. There were two things that had to be done: he must ensure the safety of Aentarra, and he must make certain that Lukaan never attained the High Seat.

With his last thoughts he called forth a force that had not been used in centuries, a force that most believed was only a tale to frighten children.

Lightning from his eyes struck a few of the last remaining guards, collapsing part of the shield, then his hands glowed as red as his crimson cape. A purple fire shot from Antar's fingers, carving a path straight to Bolledar. Reinforcements had arrived from the lower floor, but the chains of fire sliced through them like a knife through a cloud.

Perhaps Vellana recognized the aberration from her study of the histories. With no power to stop it, she leapt clear of its path. "Manacles of Light!" Her coarse whisper frightened Chandra, who could be seen shuddering from across the room.

The manacles wrapped around Bolledar's neck, then tendrils of purple flame bored into his body, his eyes, mouth, heart. He cried for help, a plea so pitiful that one of the Lights started to move, but Vellana stopped them.

"There is nothing to do for him now." Soon, Bolledar's body raged with purple fire as a blinding light erupted from within him. When it was gone, so too, was Bolledar.

The manacles turned, exhibiting a prescience not unlike the *slicers*, and cleaved a new path toward Lukaan. As they raced to their new target, Vellana shook again. "Beware the tentacles."

The manacles sliced through Lukaan's defenses and attached to him like a Gorshan Eel, but worse—cutting off a limb would not alleviate this problem.

Lukaan screamed as the manacles infiltrated his body. The chamber gasped when three tentacles shot from his heart, racing through the mass of people until they found Antar's daughters.

A father's smile was never so broad. Now their fates were intertwined —what happened to one happened to all. Now, the Lights could not make Lukaan the Light of Lights. More importantly, they could not kill his daughters without killing Lukaan. And if banishment was in the plans, Lukaan would suffer exile with them—and be there to protect them.

With that done, Antar returned to the Lights. He knew he must kill them, but they had not waited death like lambs.

Chandra seized the Book. The remaining Lights joined hands and opened it. A golden stream of light erupted, forcing them back.

Vellana stumbled.

"Do not break the chain," Chandra shouted. "We must be as one."

As they tried to rejoin hands, the Book unleashed a ferocious storm of lightning in chaotic, unrestrained power. Shards of jagged bolts erupted from the book, raging out of control. The Lights struggled to rein it in with shields but pockets of raw energy breached their defense. Walls cracked, columns buckled then fell. A guard who came too close vanished—vaporized by the power.

"Join hands and focus on the Book," Vellana said. "We must control its power."

Doranna hesitated. "It is too soon. We could be killed."

"We risk the Book or Antar. Hurry. Even now he breaks free." The fear of Antar drove them back to the Book like frightened cattle. When their four hands touched, the power was released.

Therram was the last guard to fall, a blast from Antar's lightning accelerating his demise, but though Antar was now free, he feared he might be too late.

He saw the light building in them, burning through them like a sun. He remembered the feeling from so long ago, the exultation and euphoria of so much power, and though he despised the Lights with every breath he took, he envied them this moment.

Antar knew his only chance was to strike before their power became too great. The *ergonds* screamed as he leapt to challenge the Lights. *Blackfire* shot from both hands, while bolts of *blacklightning* flew from his eyes.

Inside the Great Hall

It took only a fraction of a second for the attack to reach them, and not half so long for Antar to realize the futility of it all. With the Book as a power source, they were an invincible mass of energy and absorbed his attack as a sun would a single flame.

The Lights' fear vanished, replaced by the headiness of power.

"Antar du Savarra, Light of Lights, Eternal Flame, Keeper of the Light —we sentence you to eternal darkness. We sentence you to death."

Chandra's laughter could be heard above the others. They wove a massive shield into a whirling blade of death and dispatched it.

The shield Antar constructed was meant to withstand the force of thousands, but their weapon sliced through it like rotting melon. Antar knew it was over. He stood erect. Death should be greeted with a smile.

THE SACRED BOOK

$\mathcal{A}$entarra screamed when her father's head toppled to the floor. She could not help but cry. But even as his head came to rest on the cold floor of the chamber, she plotted.

"I will avenge you, father. I will never forget what they have done."

Her whisper went unnoticed by all but Mikkellana, eldest of Antar's daughters. "You will forget about everything other than obeisance until we are sentenced, little sister, lest the same fate befall you."

It took a while for the chamber to settle down, and even longer for the Lights to seal the Book shut again; power such as that was not constrained without great effort.

"Now we must address the issue of how to deal with those waiting to be tried." Chandra leaned toward her fellow Lights to confer, then turned to face the crowd. She looked out over the dead as if they weren't there. What did the dead matter to her, they would be gone before the night fell, replaced by more nameless, faceless guards.

"We have decided," she said. "Lukaan, take your place among your people so that the sentence may be read."

Lukaan cursed Antar as he rejoined his officers on the lower level. Even in death Antar had managed to defeat him. Lukaan looked down at his chest, the chains no longer visible but he must have felt them tugging at him with every breath.

Guards filtered in from all levels and from corridors that branched off every turn until the original one thousand had been replaced. Chandra waited until Lukaan was in place. "Warriors of Nelstar, for your crimes against the people, we sentence you to banishment. You shall serve your time in the Forbidden Lands."

Lukaan's roar shook the walls as he unleashed a full assault aimed at the Lights. But they had been prepared. The guards had woven a shield around the one hundred, anticipating Lukaan's attack. After dispersing the assault, the Lights wove a Shield of Death around Aentarra.

"Stop, Lukaan. Move against us and we kill her. You are joined by the manacles. As Aentarra's fate goes, so goes yours, or so Vellana says. But I feel certain you know the histories as well as she does."

Lukaan shifted glares between the Lights and Aentarra. She was gasping for breath, as he was now. Despite his struggle to breathe, he managed to get out, "You said banishment, but to go to the Forbidden Lands means death. You know what awaits us there."

"Nothing in the laws dictate where banishment will be served. We chose the Forbidden Lands, as is our right."

"You chose a coward's way to deliver a death verdict," Lukaan said. "No one has ever survived the Forbidden Lands."

"Yes, there is that," Chandra said, then she signaled the other Lights. "Stand by the Book. We might have need."

On the lower floor, where the one hundred stood, a door that had not been opened in centuries cracked its seal. Lukaan's chiseled face tensed. His jaw clenched. Fire ran rampant through his eyes. He turned to Aentarra, now released from the shield, then to Mikkellana, a leader among her faction. "We could fight here," he said.

Mikkellana, ever the pillar of logic and fortitude, wasted no time responding. "We would all die. You saw the power of the Book; you've tasted it yourself. All it takes is for one of us to be killed and all touched by the manacles die. Logic says we should take our chances in the Forbidden Lands."

Aentarra stared at the bodies scattered throughout the room. There was very little bloodshed, a few trickles that ran down faces of the guards or down their necks. A few uniforms stained, some smears on the marble floor. Aside from that, little to show for a battle of this magnitude. Little to tell of the thousand or so who died.

"We can come back for the Lights another time," Aentarra said. Her mouth twisted with vengeance. "They must pay for what they did to father."

"I'm afraid, little sister, you must throw that notion away. No one has ever returned from the Forbidden Lands."

Aentarra forced herself to go numb, focused on the all-important task. She recalled the image of her father as he fell, the love in his eyes. All other thoughts and images vanished. When nothing else remained, she began the recital:

"An oath of life I swear by Blood, to be—"

"No! Aentarra, no!" Mikkellana hollered as she lunged for her. She shook her and slapped Aentarra, to no avail. All she could do now was listen as Aentarra repeated the oath that was necessary for the bonding.

> *"An oath of life I swear by Blood, to be an oath of death,*
> *And each page of the Sacred Book I whisper with each breath.*
> *To the Seven Lights of Nelstar—this day I swear your death."*

Mikkellana shook her head as she pulled Aentarra to her in a warm embrace. "You should not have done that, little sister. That oath will likely be what kills you."

Aentarra stepped away without a word, and Mikkellana shuddered, most likely at the smirk on her sister's face. It was a twisted smile identical to Antar's.

"I'll come back, Mikkellana. The Lights have not rid themselves of me." As Aentarra's glare settled on the Lights, the *slicer* in her mind shivered with excitement.

Meanwhile, Mikkellana cast wary glances ahead, searching for indications of trouble. It was an inhospitable place to be sure.

Forbidden Lands as seen from the gateway in the Great Hall

As the one hundred funneled through the portal, the remaining Lights looked down with smiles, Chandra's, perhaps, the brightest of all. "After so long, we bid riddance to our two biggest problems—Antar and Lukaan."

If Chandra's smile had been the brightest, Vellana's was the broadest. "Even better, we have blessed the Forbidden Lands with Lukaan's presence." She shivered as she said it. "If anything lives there other than those beasts, I offer my sympathies for burdening them with Lukaan."

"Yes," Chandra said. "I even feel for the beasts. Pity the creatures that must share a world with him."

~

Antar's mind floated above the Chamber of Lights. He saw things with more clarity now; death had freed him from the grip of madness—from the Others. But even as he cursed them, he realized that they had been his salvation. If not them it would surely have been Her. At least he had saved the people, at least that.

But where goes Lukaan? What will become of the world he seeds? I only pray to the Makers that he stays in the Forbidden Lands, even if it means my Aentarra must stay with him. Even that is better than setting him free on another world.

"Did you not kill a world? There are worlds with less people than Nagasha."

Antar shuddered. *Where had the thought come from? Who had dared address him that way?*

It was then he felt the presence slithering through his mind. The Others were still with him. They had followed him across the threshold of death, haunted him even on this side of the Path.

But how? Did not the Makers guard the gate?

When he could not find the Makers, Antar steepled his hands and formed his lips in supplication.

"Was it not your promise that salvation awaited those who held true? Why is my mind not free? Why are the Others still with me?" Antar waited, but no response came.

Where are the Makers? What has become of them?

EXILE

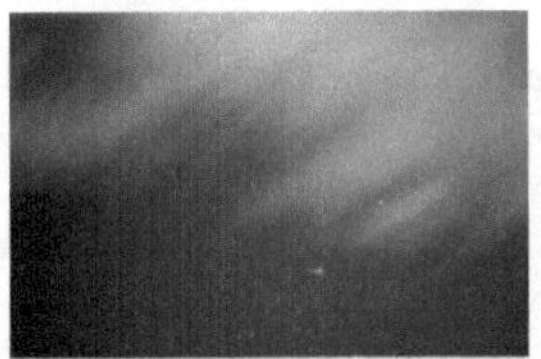

Forbidden Lands
364 AE (After Exile)
No moons to see
Third Calendar of Light

Aentarra studied the landscape as they walked. Birds—vultures they looked like—hid behind rocks waiting for them to pass so they could feed on what was left of the skeletal remains of…something.

In the distance, mountains hid the source of what appeared to be clouds rising from the floor of this desert-like land, but the clouds seemed to be filled with blood. This place put the Bharan Desert to shame, made it seem to be a vacation spot by comparison.

Perhaps the red tainting those clouds is the blood of the dorgans, Aentarra thought, then added. *I hope so.*

She stepped on something hot, hot enough to burn through her shoes. It elicited a curse. Not the first since entering these lands; not even the first since she broke fast upon waking.

It was no wonder. The ground they had been traveling over held no moisture. It was parched and cracked, and looked as if it hadn't rained in many years, possibly centuries.

For a moment, she wondered how *anything* could live in these lands, even the skeletal bodies they were passing. But then she reminded herself of the dorgans.

Landscape of Forbidden Lands

The reddened clouds had piqued her curiosity, but before it could be sated the dorgans attacked. They had been hiding behind a small enclave of rocks east of their path, and they attacked with no warning. Though no warning is what Aentarra had come to expect.

She had heard reports from long ago, during the Darkness Wars, but experiencing it firsthand was another matter.

Most of the people here had fought them during the wars, but Aentarra hadn't; she had been too young. She did, however, recall hearing discussions about them while others spoke in the meeting room.

People were firing Lightning and BlackFire at them, but it was having little effect, although there were so many of them, it was difficult to tell.

Finally, Mikkellana announced a new strategy. "Focus on one at a time," she said. "They seem to be absorbing our individual attacks, but perhaps they will not fare so well if we combine them."

The dorgans were still far away, though they were advancing rapidly. "How do we isolate which ones to go after?" Sarukh asked.

It only took Mikkellana a moment to come up with an answer. "I'll use an illumination shield," she said. "When you see the glow of the shield, it means it has attached to one of them. As soon as you see the shield light up, fire. If everyone fire at once, we have a good chance of killing them."

This was a new tactic for Aentarra. She had never heard of an illumination shield, but she was new to battle, so it was not unexpected.

Mikkellana focused her illumination on the frontrunners, the ones who led the charge, and—like most of Mikkellana's tactics—it was proving to be successful. Dorgans were falling like saplings during a Gorshan storm. During it all, the sky overhead had turned a fiery red, almost as if it were bleeding.

Fiery skies

The battle raged for hours, both sides losing warriors. Thankfully, the dorgans lost more. By nightfall, the attack was over. Despite the dorgans having retreated, Aentarra and her people were far from safe, as Mikkellana's continual reminders made clear.

"There can be no rest. Everyone must remain alert, and I mean fully alert. That means you need to sleep with a sensitivity shield at all times. If you can't weave a sensitivity shield, ask someone who can to help. This is no time for pride to interfere. Be prepared—or die."

Mikkellana's warnings had effect, and by late that night, all the survivors had found a place to rest—either against the cliff or in an enclave of seemingly protective rocks.

~

Aentarra's breath came in ragged gasps, chest heaving, body trembling. The charred gray rock of the cliffs hugged her back, the precipice rising twenty or thirty spans above the canyon floor—blood, entrails, and other matter clinging to jagged tors like primordial ooze. At the edge of the camp and beyond, smoke leaked from the cores of downed trees. Flames tickled the bark on the few left standing. No matter where she cast her gaze, no life greeted her, save that of her companions.

land devoid of life

Her gaze swept the battlefield. Bodies lay strewn about the landscape as if they had fallen from the sky, arms rent from sockets, legs severed at the knees or ankles. A scowl formed on her face as the acrid stench of spilled guts and shredded bowels swirled in the air and drifted through the camp, stinging her singed nostrils as it passed. Molten rock coagulated around the beasts' flesh—they didn't burn, just festered like boiling sludge.

The ground surrounding Lukaan shivered with unnatural cold. Aentarra tucked her hands inside her sleeves, thin lips quivering. *Coldfire!* She had not seen it since her father had used it during the Darkness, and she had been but a child then.

"How much longer?" She stared at a crowded sky, distant stars vying for recognition with refulgent lights flickering in the dark void. Aentarra shook her head, recognizing none of these stars from her youth. She wiped the blood matting her dark hair, then tied her hair behind her head. A rock became a seat, and a torn sleeve served as a cloth to wipe smudges and clean dirt from the wounds on her face. A small shield served as a makeshift bandage for the most severe wound until a healer arrived.

Forbidden Lands sky at night

Mikkellana finished healing Xanthes, who nearly had an arm severed, then she made her way to Aentarra. She twisted her head, inspecting the wounds before pulling some debris from the cuts—splinters of rock and wood.

"Keep still," Mikkellana said. "This sliced to the bone and there's still a piece of claw in here." She cleaned the cut, stanched it, then stood on wobbly legs, wiping blood-tainted sweat from her own brow.

"Make sure you fix my face."

"I don't have time for your vanity, little sister. Learn to heal it yourself or go seduce some fool to do it for you. Try Mesan; he stiffens every time you pass within a span of him."

Mikkellana shook her head and scowled. "Besides, there are others who need healing in this camp."

"You'd heal them before me?"

"I heal whoever needs it. When those beasts come back, you'll be thankful for the power of Lukaan's camp. We couldn't do it alone."

Aentarra lay with her eyelids half open. When it was time for supper, she ate, then joined those standing watch. She paced the lines with Rymel and Xanthes, eyes alert for danger but keeping a watch on others too. The eighty of them that remained guarded the fires. A few slept, collapsed from exhaustion, but the rest had not closed their eyes in days, knowing they dare not sleep.

Mikkellana approached with a new plan, yet another design of shield. "We can try these columnar shapes interspersed with reinforced wedges. If we can force those beasts to crowd into channels, the targets become easier. If we can force them into channels narrow enough, there will be no need for illumination."

"What's wrong with the illumination?" Aentarra asked. "It worked before."

Mikkellana turned in her direction. "Yes, it worked, but it took the efforts of several of our best shielders. Their powers could have been put to better use."

Xanthes shook his head. "This is not the time to experiment. The last time—"

"The last time we lost twenty lives," Mikkellana said. "We can ill afford more."

"It's a waste of time," Aentarra said.

"Nothing is a waste of time if it saves a life."

Aentarra spun to see Lukaan. Lightning sparked across her fingertips. "Since when do you care about anyone's life but your own?"

Lukaan locked gazes with her. "I see a lot of Antar in your eyes. Is that why he doted on you?"

She advanced slowly, never shifting her focus, not even blinking. "Don't you—"

"This gets us nowhere," Mikkellana said, and lay a soothing hand on her sister's shoulder. "We have more important issues to deal with, and if we don't come up with something new they'll wear away at us until no one is left. Remember, sister, all they have to do is kill one of us attached to the manacles, and we all go."

"Precisely what I came to discuss," Lukaan said. "The manacles."

"They stay on." Lightning danced in Aentarra's palms. Ready.

"Easy, sister, we can hear what he has to say."

"Look at how many we have lost already," Lukaan said. "The beasts are strong. If—"

"I'm not worried about my own life, Lukaan. If you have nothing new to say, we will keep things as they are. As to Aentarra, I'll protect her. You take care of our other sister. And if they get you… I will consider my own life a fair trade."

"It would be wiser to unleash them. No harm will visit any of you. I'll even take an oath."

Aentarra brushed Mikkellana's hand from her shoulder. She had calmed herself, though it still felt as if fires danced in her eyes. "The same oath you took as a Light? The same pledge that you gave to our father?"

Muscles tensed on Lukaan's strong Runellan face, and his eyes turned red. "You *are* Antar's brat. I can see that now, but don't forget that I'm not cursed with the du Savarra vengeance. My war was with your father, not you or your sister."

Mikkellana stepped between them. "Perhaps we should discuss this later. There are points to be considered on both sides and we—"

"There is nothing to discuss. Unleashing the manacles requires all four of us to agree. And you'll never get my vote."

Mikkellana spun and grabbed her sister's throat as quick as an Asoran viper. "You'll vote as I say, little sister, or I'll lock you in a shield with air enough to breathe, no more. Death will be your fondest dream."

"We can't trust him. Look what happened to father."

Lukaan clenched his fists, taking a step forward. "As I said, Aentarra, the du Savarra blood doesn't taint my veins. Vengeance does not drive my every breath. Besides, I need all of you. None of us can shield, and without that protection the beasts would have us in no time."

"Then we'll die together," Aentarra said.

"An oath, you said." Mikkellana stared at Lukaan. "If you take an oath of life and death that neither you nor your people will harm any of us, even try to harm us, and I will consider unleashing the manacles."

"This is a mistake, Mikkellana."

Lukaan locked gazes with Mikkellana. "I will take the oath, but only for myself and only for you and Aentarra. I cannot guarantee what others may or may not do, though I doubt you have reason to fear any of them. None of them can stand against you, Mikkellana. Not even Ghruehne or Tirzinitzia."

"Don't do it," Xanthes said, having just joined the conversation. "He can't be trusted."

"He hasn't killed you yet. He could have killed all of you during these many years, yet he didn't. Stay out of this, Xanthes. It doesn't concern you." Mikkellana stood in silence for a few moments, then nodded. "Agreed then. You take the oath and we will unleash the manacles."

Lukaan called Melissara to join them, then he swore the oath in front of the three du Savarra sisters.

> "An oath of life I swear by blood to be an oath of death
> If ever I first draw du Savarra blood,
> Let it be with my last breath."

"That leaves you some measure of freedom," Mikkellana said.

"I need protection from you as well. This way I'm free to retaliate."

"I won't break my word, Lukaan. I never have, and I never—"

Lukaan nodded to Aentarra, eyes aflame and lightning sparking between her fingers. "She's the one I'm concerned about. Her blood came straight from Antar. If she didn't have Molina's eyes and hair, I'd swear she was birthed from his blood alone."

"I'll take care of Aentarra. Now let's be done with this."

They proceeded with the unleashing, and as the last words were spoken, a crimson image of the manacles appeared in the air between them, purple tentacles stretching to each of their hearts. Aentarra felt the pressure release from her chest, pressure she had not realized was even there until it was gone. Now, though, she felt free. A smile stretched her thin lips wide as she directed her scathing glare at Lukaan. *One day...*

～

Two days passed with few opportunities to sleep. During a break Aentarra rested with her back against the cliff, head buried in her hands.

"What's wrong, sister? Are you ill?"

"It's nothing."

"You might brush off a stranger with that, but I know you. Pain has never found fertile ground in your body... yet I could have sworn I saw the identical expression I used to see on father's face. That look of agony." Silence followed. "Here, let me heal you. It—"

"I'll tend to my own problems." Aentarra braced herself against the rocks as she rose, trembling, then stalked away.

"A fine alliance this is. Keep it up and it won't be long before the beasts have us."

Aentarra made her way to the front line, joining Xanthes and the others already on watch.

Night fell like a blanket over them, smothering both the light and the soothing sounds that accompanied it. Aentarra stared into the eerie darkness, watching the flames dance on logs. Not being able to see was bad, but worst of all was the unnatural silence. She never imagined silence could be so frightening.

Mikkellana approached with Lukaan and Rymel. Her dire admonitions offered no relief. "Lukaan, Xanthes, Rymel. I forewarned when they would strike the last time, but no one listened. Pay heed now. They *will* return. I feel them out there."

Aentarra shuddered. Something in Mikkellana's tone held the ominous edge of certainty. The fear was pervasive, clinging to anxious whispers that rumbled through the encampment.

"Enough!" Lukaan's bellow stirred the angst building in all of them. "It serves no purpose to fight here. We must prepare to—"

The attack came without warning.

One of the enemy seized Rymel before anyone could react. Huge claws slashed across her chest, rending flesh. A howl pierced the night, escaping her lips just before the beast ripped her face apart. Blood and other matter splattered on Aentarra's face.

"Rymel!" She screamed, cleaning herself off with one hand while *blacklightning* shot from the other.

The furor of the attack incited the encampment, and they unleashed their powers. The night sky streaked with lightning, striking the enemy in an unremitting barrage, and the air cracked with fire, engulfing them in flame; yet still they came—numberless armies with no care for death.

Lightning

Splashes of light punctured the air, turning darkness to day. Hordes of the enemy appeared on the hilltops then rushed forward in an endless sweep. More emerged from what remained of the forest, trees still weeping smoke from the previous onslaught.

Mikkellana forged an impregnable shield, but the enemy pressed the weight of the attack against the barrier until it, too, displayed signs of weakening. Soon, cracks developed.

"I cannot hold much longer. We must retreat." Fear was an emotion long since lost on Mikkellana, but tonight it laced her tone like ivy on the ancient walls of Endora.

Lukaan's roar exploded in the darkness. At times, he seemed more beast than man. *Blacklightning* shot from his fingers, drinking the light and destroying every hideous beast it touched, and Coldfire erupted from his hands, shattering their lurid bodies. It was a prodigious demonstration of power, slaying thousands of the enemy, though when Lukaan exhausted his powers, their numbers seemed no less; the onslaught continued unabated.

More of them joined Rymel as shields buckled and cracked, leaving gaping holes in the defense. A glimmering mist appeared in the darkness behind them, a shadow shivering at dawn's light. The glow caught Aentarra's eye, and she risked a glance backward.

It must be a portal.

New life replenished her depleting powers. They had searched so long, and this was one of the few portals they had seen, though none of the others had been so close. Hope blossomed in her heart, a chance that perhaps this one would not vanish like the others. "Mikkellana, a portal."

Mikkellana spun to see the unnatural mist hovering within the camp. "Xanthes, Mesan, all of you, help with a shield. We might hold them off long enough to escape."

They constructed the most intricate shield they could—with diminished powers—mixing columns, domes, and other time-proven shapes. Once completed, the entire force hastened to reach the portal, hope clinging to every labored breath.

When they breached the barrier, Mikkellana wove another shield.

"Hurry and help me seal it, all of you. No one must ever go there again."

Mikkellana faced Lukaan. "What do we do now? We've found a new world, a new start. I don't know what this world holds for us, but I believe we have a chance to begin anew. Rather than quarrel, I think we should go our separate ways and take that opportunity."

"Do what you want, Mikkellana. Just stay out of my way," Lukaan said.

Aentarra's eyes narrowed and fire danced on the tips of her fingers.

Lukaan glared at Aentarra, then turned to Mikkellana. "And keep that imp away from me, or I'll send you her ashes."

As Lukaan and his followers departed, Aentarra turned to her sister. "I warned you not to trust him. Now we must start the battles anew and thanks to you, they have us far outnumbered."

Mikkellana sighed. "We know nothing yet, little sister. Let's wait and see what tomorrow brings."

ACKNOWLEDGMENTS

It is with great honor that I give eternal gratitude to my wife and all four of my grandkids. They give me the inspiration to keep going.

ABOUT THE AUTHOR

Giacomo Giammatteo is the author of gritty crime dramas about murder, mystery, and family. He also writes non-fiction books including the No Mistakes Careers series, No Mistakes Publishing, No Mistakes Grammar, and No Mistakes Writing.

When Giacomo isn't writing, he's helping his wife take care of the animals on their sanctuary. At last count they had forty-five animals—eleven dogs, a horse, six cats, and twenty-six pigs.

Oh, and one crazy—and very large—wild boar, who takes walks with Giacomo every day and happens to also be his best buddy.

nomistakespublishing.com
gg@giacomog.com

Blood Flows South Series:

A Bullet For Carlos: A Connie Gianelli Mystery

Finding Family, a Novella

A Bullet From Dominic

Redemption Series:

Necessary Decisions: A Gino Cataldi Mystery

Old Wounds

Promises Kept, the Story of Number Two

Premeditated

OTHER BOOKS COMING SOON:

You can always see the current and coming-soon books on my website.

Fiction:

A Promise of Vengeance **(Fantasy)**

My first fantasy, and the first book in a four-book series—the Rules of Vengeance. (Three are already written and the fourth is being outlined.)

A Hard Life, the Story of Tip Denton

Memories for Sale **(mystery/sf)**

The Joshua Citadel **(SF novella)**

Nonfiction:

Whiskers and Bear—Volume I of the Life on the Farm Series (sent to editor)

No Mistakes Writing, How to Write a Bestseller

Children's Books:

No Mistakes Grammar for Kids, Volume I—Much and Many (sent to editor)

No Mistakes Grammar for Kids, Volume II—Lie and Lay (sent to editor)

No Mistakes Grammar for Kids, Volume III—Then and Than (sent to editor)

Shinobi Goes to School—Life on the Farm for kids. (working on illustrations)

Get on the mailing list and you'll be sure to be notified of release dates and sales.

<u>Mailing list</u>

And don't forget to leave a review!

By the way, if you're an author and you liked the formatting in this book, you might consider us for your next book. Information can be obtained here.

9 781940 313603